Theseus

by Simon Spence

Artwork by Colm Lawton

Copyright: Early Myths

First Edition

First Published 2017

ISBN: 978-1981825103

For Eimear + Eva

Welcome...

We hope you enjoy our story of the Greek hero Theseus.

For more information about the series and to listen to the pronunciation of the names, visit:
www.earlymyths.com
(sometimes grown-ups find these challenging but kids love them!)

Also, check out our books on the Apple iBooks Store & the Amazon Kindle Store.

For news of our current books or new titles, visit our website, follow us on Twitter or like us on Facebook!

w: www.earlymyths.com
t: @EarlyMyths
f: www.facebook.com/EarlyMyth/

Theseus

There once was a boy called Theseus who grew up without knowing his father. King Aegeus had travelled home to the great city of Athens, but before he left he placed a sword and a pair of sandals under a huge rock, ready for the day that Theseus became a man. But would Theseus ever grow up to be strong enough to lift the big rock- it was huge!

As he learnt to run, to hunt and to fight in battle, his strength grew. One day, with the help of the magical goddess Athena, he pulled the rock up from the ground to reveal the gifts. He said goodbye to his home and began his long journey to finally meet his father.

As Theseus set out on his travels, he realised he would meet many strange and menacing people on the road to Athens. The path was dangerous and it would take all of his power and his bravery to reach Athens safely.

The first man he met was the evil club-bearer, Periphetes. This bearded-man would hide behind rocks and bash passers-by on the head with his wooden club. As Periphetes jumped out at Theseus, the hero grabbed the weapon from his hand and punished him with a thump on his head. Periphetes fell to the ground, dazed by Theseus' strength, and our hero passed on by.

As Theseus travelled along the road into the mountains, he knew he needed to watch out for sneaky Sinis. This man would catch anyone walking near his home, tie their leg to the branch of a bendy tree, and then let go, hurling them across the valley to the far side.

But Theseus was ready. He grabbed the rogue by his arm and even as Sinis stretched with his hand to try to hold onto a large rock, Theseus tied Sinis with his own ropes and suddenly let go of the branch. This sent poor Sinis hurtling into the air and over to the hills beyond. Brave Theseus continued, walking on towards Athens.

As Theseus travelled through the forest he heard a rustling from the bushes. He watched carefully for wild bears and boars, with his hand on his sword and his eyes on the path. Quick as a dart, out rushed the sow of Krommyon, a thundering and snorting pig-beast.

Theseus dived to one side as the creature tried to bite him, narrowly avoiding a nasty nip. The sow's owner was an old woman who stood by and refused to call it back.

Each time the sow appeared from the bushes, Theseus struck it with his sword, until it collapsed quietly on the forest floor.

After his narrow escape, Theseus climbed along a rocky path beside the deep sea. Here he met Skiron, who asked travellers for help. Skiron begged Theseus to pour water into his bowl and help to wash his sore feet. Theseus felt sorry for the man but as he bent down to mix the cool water and began to bathe the weary feet, Skiron started his tricks. He lifted his foot and tried to push Theseus off the cliff, down towards a giant crab beneath. Quick-thinking Theseus grabbed Skiron by his ankle, swung him around and flung him towards the water. Theseus heard the snap, snap of crab claws as he hurried away and continued his travels towards Athens.

"Be careful on the road Theseus" said goddess Athena, who watched over all the heroes. "Use your mind and use your strength to take on anyone who challenges you."

Theseus walked on and saw a man standing on the path. This was the wrestler Kerkyon. Theseus did not want to fight him but Kerkyon would not let anyone pass until they wrestled with him. Theseus warned him but Kerkyon was too stubborn. "Fight me!" he grunted and so Theseus took hold and locked arms. The two men gripped and grappled until Theseus held Kerykon in the air and dropped him to the ground, winning the contest with his strength and skills.

After all of his challenges, Theseus finally arrived at the great city of Athens. He entered the doorway of the palace to speak to his father for the first time. "I am King Aegeus" said his father "and you are most welcome to my home."

But not everyone was so happy to see Theseus! The other royal princes were jealous. They muttered in the corners of the great hall and at dinner time they dropped a poisonous mix into his cup, just as King Aegeus was about to celebrate with his visitor. As Theseus raised the drink to his lips, Aegeus saw the devious look in the princes' eyes and knocked the cup from Theseus' hand.

Saved from the poison, Theseus sat with the King and the old man told a sad tale: "A prince from the island of Crete once came to our land but died here in an accident. The King of Crete demanded a punishment and each year we must send a ship with seven boys and seven girls to face a fierce creature, the Minotaur."

Theseus was shocked and decided this must stop. He begged that he be one of the boys so he could break this curse. King Aegeus sadly agreed but made him promise that he would take down the ship's black sails if he came home safely. Aegeus watched as the boat departed, hoping to see white sails and his son again soon.

Each of the other boys and girls were terrified- none of them had faced the adventures that Theseus had gone through.

Theseus spoke to King Minos when they arrived at Crete. Minos agreed that Theseus could go down into the labyrinth first, the dark and twisting passages where the Minotaur lived. The creature was half man, half bull and would charge at anyone who journeyed into the labyrinth's many paths. King Minos' daughter, princess Ariadne, listened to Theseus and she began to fall in love with the hero. She gathered a ball of thread and kept it safe; she had a plan which could help Theseus.

That night, Ariadne spoke to Theseus: "take this thread with you, tie it to the door as you enter the labyrinth and unwind it as you move along the dark paths."

Next morning, Theseus took his sword and entered the doorway, slowly unravelling the thread as he went, until he could hear the heavy breathing of the beast. He arrived to face the Minotaur at the heart of the labyrinth and it let out a roar and charged at Theseus. He leapt into the air and somersaulted over its back. Each time he jumped high, just as the beast reached him, until it grew slow and tired. The curse was ended as the beast finally collapsed on the ground.

Theseus grabbed the ball of thread and gathered it back up as he followed the right path through the twisting labyrinth all the way back to the doorway, and to the waiting princess. Ariadne warned him that they must escape quickly, as it would not be long before King Minos found out about his precious Minotaur.

Ariadne, Theseus and the other boys and girls from Athens rushed to the boat. As they put up the sails, Minos and his army rushed towards the harbour but they were too late- Theseus steered the boat away from Crete and safely out to sea. The curse was broken and Theseus sailed the crew towards Athens.

But it was not meant to be...

Theseus and his crew stopped at an island for food and water on the long journey home. The goddess Athena had decided that Ariadne would not travel to Athens with Theseus, and their lives were not meant to be together.

Instead, the playful god Dionysus took Ariadne away to celebrate with his friends and Athena told Theseus to think about his home and his family, as he sailed away from the island. Athena knew that Theseus was to be a great king one day and she needed him to prepare for what lay ahead.

Theseus missed Ariadne at first but began to think about his home and the joy of seeing his father again. However, he had forgotten one very important thing! He had made a promise to King Aegeus before he set sail for Crete; he promised to change the sails from black to white so the king would see he was safe as the ship sailed over the horizon and towards the harbour. But when King Aegeus stood looking out to sea that morning, he saw black sails returning. King Aegeus turned away, sure that his son had died at Crete and he fell from the walls of the city with a broken heart.

When Theseus and the crew arrived home, they found a city sad with the loss of their king.

Even after all of his adventures and troubles, Theseus decided to go on one more journey, this time to the Underworld where the ghosts of the dead lived. His friend Peirithoos foolishly believed he could marry Persephone, Queen of the Underworld, and so they travelled into the dark kingdom.

But Hades, King of the Underworld, heard about their plan and as he welcomed them to his home, he used magic to trap their wrists and feet to their chairs. Theseus wondered if they would ever escape! Luckily his friend Herakles soon came passing by. He was there to borrow Cerberus, Persephone's dog, and as he was leaving he spotted his friend and freed him from his chains.

Theseus had had a lucky escape and decided to return home to Athens. There was trouble at the city and after all of his adventures it was now time for him to become their king. Armies were marching towards Athens and Theseus led his people in battles, winning wars and making the city the biggest and most important town in the land. From now on, King Theseus decided that every four years a great parade would be held to show the world about the greatness of his city.

Theseus had triumphed in many adventures but now he was the mighty king of the greatest city in the world.

THE END

Some interesting notes for grown-ups...

Notes About The Myth:

Theseus' tale is about the foundation of a city and it has many parallels to the stories of Jason and Perseus and their adventures on their journeys. The episodic nature of Theseus' adventures is similar to the labours of Herakles. Our hero faces creatures and dangerous people and must overcome each obstacle with a mix of strength and guile. Sinis, with his bendy branches and his tricking of passers-by is an example of this.

490-480 BC, Staatliche Antikensammlungen, Munich

c.525-475 BCE, Ashmolean Museum, Oxford

For both Sinis and the Minotaur, we followed the original Greek vase paintings closely as both tales were frequently represented in art and the depictions of the characters are so vivid.

In our choice for the Minotaur we had to decide which position to choose as there are examples of Theseus in different poses. We went for the moment with most impact - the struggle as he holds the beast's horns as it tires and falls to the ground.

c.490 BCE, British Museum, London

One last example from art is this beautiful vase from the British Museum, which contains many of the stories of Theseus in its central panel. At the middle is Theseus with the defeated Minotaur. Working clockwise from the top is Theseus along with: Kerkyon, Prokrustes (not in our tale), Skiron, the Bull of Marathon (not included here), Sinis, and the Sow. Our images closely follow the examples on this vase and others from this period.

c.440-430 BCE, British Museum, London

Printed in Great Britain
by Amazon